A MAN OF
HUMBLE AGE

A MAN OF
HUMBLE AGE

Kana Ugess

First paperback edition 2023

Lyrics by Haven Emrys

978-1-80541-120-8 (paperback)
978-1-80541-121-5 (ebook)

www.kanaugess.com

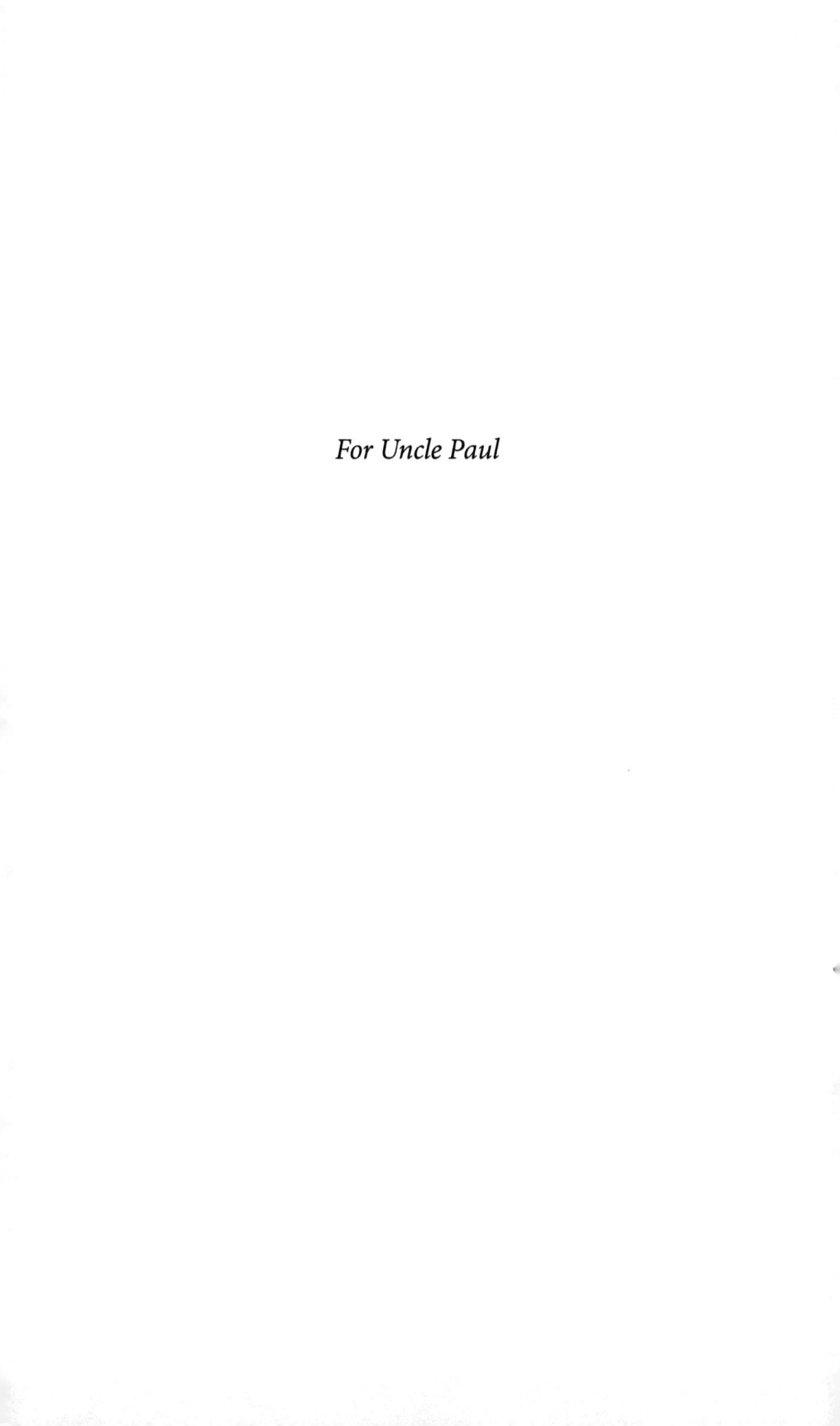

For Uncle Paul

CONTENTS

CHAPTER 1

PRESENT DAY

The mimosa trees stood proudly in front of the white marble steps and columns, the sunlight reflecting around the open garden courtyard and upon the converted manor house. The golden gravel crunched under the wheels as the first of the day's expected guests arrived.

Shutting the door of his Mercedes CLK, Martin stood looking up at the feigned grandeur before him. His white suit gleamed in the light as much as his blue silk shirt contrasted it. He slowly removed his sunglasses as he marched up the steps, opting to hang them from his open collar instead of on top of his thinning sandy hair.

A plump figure bustled out of the doorway, dressed in grey from her short-cropped hair to her patent leather court shoes. "Mr Acton!"

"Ms Doherty." Martin took her outstretched hand in his and gave a solemn smile. "I had hoped we'd meet on better terms."

"Unfortunately, that's not normally the case in my line of work." She motioned for him to proceed before her as they entered the main reception hall. "Though this is actually a first for me in my many years of being here."

"Well, you can thank Rob for that." Martin laughed heartily as he signed the visitor book and followed her through to a large room marked as the Sun Lounge by a wooden plaque on the door.

Inside sat two women chatting animatedly with each other as they tenderly held hands. They were as different as chalk and cheese, one being rather stout and fair whilst the other was slight and tanned. Both, Martin noted, had extraordinary hair colours.

"Martin, this is Jess and Ashley Lewis, two of our staff members. Jess, Ashley, this is Mr Martin Acton, Rob's executor."

"One of his executors," he corrected as he held out a hand. "It's a pleasure to finally meet you both."

"Ah, Mike!" Ms Doherty called as she beckoned to the young man in the doorway. "Good timing, this is-"

"We've met," Martin interrupted, thrusting out his hand again. "How are you, chap?"

"Still going," Mike smiled as he took Martin's hand warmly.

After all the pleasantries were exchanged and old faces were reacquainted, Martin sat down with a deep sigh. "I don't think there is much more we can do until others arrive."

"Are there many more outside parties we are expecting?" Ms Doherty asked, contemplating numbers on her fingers as she looked about the room.

"Two or three outsiders plus the residents we spoke about," Martin replied smoothly.

Ms Doherty considered the room briefly, looking at her watch before issuing commands to her staff. The tables were carried away to the walls, and the chairs pushed into four neat columns split in half by a makeshift aisle, facing the solitary sofa at the end.

Mike and Ashley left briefly to assemble the summoned residents whilst Martin went to wait for the other guests in the fresh air. Something about being back at Mimosa Grange without seeing Rob was starting to gnaw away at him.

Outside, it didn't take long before a Volvo estate pulled up, glinting dark green in the abundant sunlight. Martin watched as its driver twisted to its passenger seat and collated his belongings together before stepping out onto the gravel.

"You never travel light, do you?" Martin scoffed as he held open the front door of Mimosa Grange.

"Not wherever you and Rob are involved!"

"Ah, you'll miss us when we're gone."

"Not long to wait then," the balding gentleman replied in a monotone voice as he looked over the pile in his arms at his associate. "I'll be out of a job when you go."

"I have no plans to leave work yet, Dave!" Martin chuckled as he followed him through the building and back into the Sun Lounge.

Where once were empty chairs, there was now a bedraggled elderly group, muttering away to themselves as they watched wide-eyed and half-expectant. Martin motioned to the front of the group, where the lone sofa was still unoccupied. Dave soon claimed the area with his briefcase and the belongings he had brought in with him before turning to introduce himself as 'Mr Wright' to Ms Doherty.

Martin watched for a while, his heart tightening slightly at the active room as he realised he was searching for Rob. He sighed, checked his watch, and, with a flick of his suit jacket, left to go back outside and await the last remaining guest.

Checking his watch again, Martin pulled out a pack of cigarettes, lighting one before taking a long drag. Leaning against the stone doorway, he stared past the cigarette in his fingers as he watched the bees hovering amongst the flowers.

"I thought you gave up that habit?" Mr Wright remarked as he approached sullenly.

"You'd take up the habit if you knew who we were expecting," Martin sighed as he crushed the end of his butt in his fingertips.

"I may not know her as personally as you, but I certainly know who I'm expecting."

"And just that knowledge still hasn't driven you to smoke in anticipation of her?"

"No. Though it has raised questions. Rob amending the will several times over recent years hasn't helped answer any, either. Do I want to know where a retired man in a care home got that amount of money?"

"You're his other executor. How do you not know?"

"I just wanted it confirmed for my own peace of mind."

"Well, let's say Rob volunteered his musical knowledge and gifted the money raised. He was still technically retired."

"I thought that might be the case. You learned too much from him in the music industry."

"You make it sound as though we've given you a life-long headache."

"Whatever you want to believe. In any case, we can't wait too much longer; I have other appointments this afternoon."

"Couldn't get a break from being a partner of the firm for one day?"

"It doesn't work like that. I'll see you inside in ten minutes."

"As unfeeling as ever, I see," Martin called after him. "You could at least shed one tear for Rob during today's proceedings." He sniffed dryly as silence responded. Checking his watch several times, he eventually straightened himself and turned to head back in.

The crunching of the gravel sent a shiver up his spine as he froze to the spot. Quickly he pulled out another cigarette and took a shaky drag before turning to face the scene behind him.

The pale Nissan Figaro that had parked haphazardly across in front of the other cars was already grating on Martin's nerves. The passenger door opened as a rather disgruntled man in his early sixties climbed out and proceeded to lean against the side of the car. He pulled out his mobile from his pocket and began to press buttons though his face remained remarkably uninterested.

Inside the car, the woman, who unimpressed Martin more than anyone else, was applying fresh makeup and fluffing her ridiculous hair. Eventually, with a smack of her pouted lips, the woman climbed out of the car and slammed the door shut resolutely.

She tottered over the gravel in her suede heels, barely able to lift her legs in the tight lacey black dress that enclosed her. A tiny bag tattooed with branded logos clung to her elbow as she yelled at her husband to hurry up.

"Lisa," Martin acknowledged as she approached.

"We don't have time to wait for your cigarette breaks," she spat venomously as she pushed past.

Martin sighed as he rolled his eyes. He gritted his teeth, holding back all manner of obscenities. Setting his jaw straight, he stubbed out his cigarette and followed them inside.

The Sun Lounge became aptly quiet as a confident Lisa strolled in, her heels clicking against the wooden floor, her husband following silently. She took her place at the front of the rows of chairs, making a show of crossing her legs and placing her bag on the floor beside her as she sat down.

Martin shut the door and took his place at the front on the opposite side of the makeshift aisle. He sat comfortably and quietly and tried his best not to disturb Dave Wright, who had now stood to address the crowd.

"Welcome, and thank you for coming. I'd like to begin today by stating that this is a very rare occurrence that I happen to have the pleasure of witnessing. As a rule, will readings are not hosted as such, but as Mr Sallow's Solicitor and Estate Attorney, it is my duty to ensure his will is read according to his last wishes along with his chosen executor, Mr Acton." He motioned a directive hand towards Martin. "As requested, the chosen beneficiaries have been called together in one room, more specifically here, at Mimosa Grange, to aid those beneficiaries who are current residents of Mimosa Grange. Without further ado, I shall begin to read the bequests as directed by Mr Sallow.

'To Lisa, I leave to you my memories …'"

CHAPTER 2

AGED 83

Robert stepped out of the taxi and stared up at the building before him. With a shake of his head, he met the driver at the rear of the car, who was already lifting the two large suitcases out of the boot. He paid the man with a larger tip than normal because not only had he provided a well-meaning conversation along the journey, but he had also carried his belongings up the few steps to the front door. Good customer service cost nothing but should be rewarded well.

A woman met him at the front door. "Good morning; you must be Mr Sallow."

"I am." Robert nodded with a smile though he was struggling to feel positive about his being here.

"I'm Amanda Doherty, the manager here. Please just call me Amanda. If you come this way, I can show you to your room. Your daughter filled out all the paperwork, so there's nothing to worry about."

The woman was friendly but clearly authoritative and liked a well-kept schedule. She carried one of the cases in while he maintained a guarding grip on the other. Bypassing the front reception desk, she pointed down the hallway to highlight the lift before proceeding to lead the way up a flight of stairs and down a corridor to a room three doors down. His name had already been printed, laminated and attached to the wall at eye height next to the door frame.

He closed his eyes momentarily and took a deep breath. At the age of eighty-three, he still hadn't envisioned himself in such a place as Mimosa Grange. He followed Amanda, who was, exceptionally friendly and well-mannered, as she continued to explain about his room, meal times, fire exits and carers. She placed the suitcase she was carrying on top of the sideboard that stood under the window. She then returned to the doorway and called, "Mike?"

"Yes?" A man with baked-cinnamon-coloured skin appeared, slightly out of breath, clearly knowing he was a little late to meet up with them.

"Mr Sallow, this is Mike, one of our carers on shift today. He will help you settle in and show you to the Sun Lounge to meet with some of our other residents."

"Thank you." He smiled again at Amanda before she bustled away back towards her office. Robert's face relaxed as he turned to the carer before him. "I don't suppose you'd mind helping me?"

"Of course not; that's what I'm here for." Mike smiled. "Would you like me to unpack your suitcase? You can sit in the chair and rest as I do so?"

"If you could do that one on the sideboard, please, I'd rather do this one myself."

Mike gave a thumbs up with a beaming face before beginning to empty the suitcase of all its clothes, either hanging them in the wardrobe or folding them into the dresser, both of which were against the wall by the door.

Robert gently placed the case he was still holding onto the bed. He slid the latches on either side and gingerly raised the lid, holding his breath for fear that anything was out of place or damaged. With a slow exhale of relief, he pulled the record player out and placed it on top of the dresser, squaring it up neatly. He pulled out a small box of records and placed these next to the player. Returning to the case, Robert haphazardly threw music books out onto the bed and focused his attention on a small, long, thin case that he picked up and gently caressed before opening. Inside was a silver flute, shining in its polished and well-kept glory.

"Have you played long?" Mike asked, almost startling Robert.

"Since I was six."

"Wow! I bet you are amazing. My daughter has just started taking lessons, though she gets easily frustrated when she practices."

"I wouldn't say that I'm amazing." He closed the lid again with a soft click. "I'm always willing to hear her play if she wants an audience."

Mike placed the suitcase he had finished emptying inside the now empty one on the bed; then, with a swinging motion, he threw them up on top of the wardrobe so that they were out of the way. He turned back to face Robert, slapping his hands together with a job well done. "I bet Amiyah would love that, though I think your ears would be better off without." He laughed at the memory of last night's music practice.

"We all have to start somewhere," Robert remarked kindly as he began lining up his music books alphabetically.

"That's true." Mike opened another door that led to a wet room, placing the toiletries he had found in there. "Do you have any questions? About here, I mean," he quickly added.

"Will I be allowed out for good behaviour?"

"I'm afraid not, Rob. Can I call you Rob?"

Robert nodded, and Mike continued.

"You have full access to walk around from your room to the Sun Lounge, dining hall and conservatory downstairs. You can go out in the garden too, but you best let one of us know you are out there first."

Robert sighed. "But I'm not allowed back out in society on my own?"

"Unfortunately not; it's just in case something happens when you're out. We don't want something bad to happen to you now, do we?"

"I am of the understanding it already has," Robert muttered to himself.

"It's not all that bad here, honestly." Mike grinned with a small wink. "Besides, it could be worse; Amiyah could be practising for you!"

Robert smiled wistfully. "How old is she?"

"Ten and a half now; I'm not allowed to forget the half." Mike winked again.

"Ah yes, the half is very important," Robert nodded thoughtfully before they both laughed.

"Shall we head downstairs to the Sun Lounge?" Mike suggested.

"I suppose I must brave it eventually."

The two made their way slowly, continuing to discuss Amiyah and music. By the front reception desk, a sweet old lady using a wheeled Zimmer frame shuffled in their direction. She looked up, and as her eyes locked onto Robert's, her lips upturned into the biggest of grins. She raised a shaky hand to catch at his arm, forcing him to stop.

"This is Dorothy Smalls," Mike introduced her. "Good morning, Dorothy. How are you today?"

"Good," she replied but never took her gaze from Robert. "Thank you."

"Dorothy, this is Robert. He's going to be staying with us from now on."

"Rob...ert." Her eyes twinkled as she repeated the name.

Without letting go of her grip on his arm, she used her other hand to fish into her pocket. She pulled out a small, crumpled white paper bag of chocolate limes and offered them to him.

"Thank you, Dorothy." Robert smiled as he took one of the wrapped sweets from the bag.

Dorothy gave a small giggle as she hid the sweets in her pocket again. With one last glance at his face, she continued on her way, the beaming smile still making its home on her face.

"I don't think I've ever seen her smile so much," Mike commented as he watched after her. "I think you've made a friend there."

"So sweet," Robert mused as he twirled the offering between his fingers before placing it in his cardigan pocket.

The Sun Lounge was a glorified reception room. One wall was full of windows that brightened the room even on the darkest of days, overlooking a small side garden full of yellow mimosas. All the armchairs were exactly the same and looked more plastic than leather. It was all rather clinical. Robert supposed it was for easy cleaning, but the thought made him feel a little queasy.

"Sat over in the corner knitting is Barbara and her son Stephen. She is rather brusque but can be a good laugh; you'll see her son coming and going nearly every day. And over there is Barry and Mathilda."

Barry waved an espresso-dark hand in their direction at the mention of his name.

"Mathilda has advanced dementia. Barry moved in here with her to be able to be near her. They're inseparable. Finally, the gentleman over there leaning over the coffee table is Dr John Hughes. You will usually find him with a book or crossword."

"Small number of residents," Robert commented to himself.

"Not all the residents like to, or can, come out of their rooms." Mike hesitated before changing the subject. "Would you like a drink? The tea trolley should be around soon. I'd love to stay and chat longer, but I still have other residents to help out."

"Don't let me stop you." Robert gently patted Mike's arm. "We've already established I won't be going anywhere."

"Sorry about that." Mike looked guilty on his behalf.

"No need." Robert waved his hand. "Could I ask, if you have time that is, that you post this for me, please?" He reached into his other pocket and pulled out a small letter.

"Of course, no problem," Mike smiled as he received the letter and disappeared back to his rounds.

Robert took a deep breath and steeled himself. He sat down next to one of the windows where he could admire the mimosas outside fluttering in the breeze or observe the other inmates locked in this overly safe, clinical jail cell of a care home. With a brief moment of remembrance, he pulled the chocolate lime back out of his pocket and smiled to himself. Maybe it wouldn't be so bad after all.

CHAPTER 3

AGED 84

66 Virulent," John exclaimed for the second time.

"Oh, sorry." Robert scribbled down the word upon the crossword before him.

"What's up, Pal?" John tapped the arm of his wheelchair twice to bring Robert's focus back to him. "You seem far away today."

Robert sighed, placing the crossword down and removing his reading glasses. "I haven't seen Barry at all today."

"Now that you mention it," John looked around the room to double-check, "I haven't either. Maybe Mathilda is having a bad day, and he's staying with her?"

Robert nodded slowly in agreement though it still bothered him. He perched his glasses on the end of his nose again. "Alone. Eight letters, fourth letter is an 'i.'" He peered over the top of his spectacles at his crossword companion.

John was a proud Scotsman about twenty-five years Robert's junior, though he looked significantly older. He had suffered a stroke which had left his already weakened body wheelchair-bound; his face was a clear indicator to anyone who saw him. His speech had improved vastly with therapy, and his mind still whirred away, though at a considerably slower pace, much to his own frustration. Even now, as Robert watched him, he could see John was tapping his one hand determinedly in an effort to remember the word that not so long ago would have just rolled off his tongue.

Robert sighed, ashamedly grateful that he was not in John's position. For an academic man of any intelligence, much more so one of high intellect, life's predicaments had a way of holding you hostage in your own body. He couldn't even begin to imagine his life without music. Being unable to play would be like chopping off his limbs and taking away his hearing aids. Not a life worth living for a musician.

John lifted a handkerchief from the chest pocket of his tweed jacket and, rather unceremoniously, due to the shakiness of his limbs, dabbed away the drool that was trying to escape from the downturned corner of his mouth.

"Grandad!" a little voice chirped as a small boy ran into the room, crashing into the side of John's wheelchair.

"Aye, Laddie," John hurriedly stuffed the handkerchief away again and patted the boy's head.

"Samuel, what did I tell you about being careful with Grandad?" came an exasperated woman's voice as she followed her son.

"Julia." John tried to smile at her, though his face clearly was unresponsive on one side.

"Dad, Robert." Julia planted a kiss on her father's head before nodding in greeting to Robert.

"Take my place." Robert raised himself out of the armchair and winked at Samuel, who was watching him.

"Thank you, Robert," Julia replied, smiling appreciatively at him. Her eyes were tired, no doubt from running after little Samuel all day. Her hair was a fantastic marigold orange, which was clearly showing itself as a family trait, along with the fields of freckles the Hughes family were blanketed with.

With another friendly smile directed at the Hughes, Robert left the Sun Lounge in search of Barry. He wasn't prepared to listen to Barbara rattle on about Stephen's last visit, and even sweet Dorothy had fallen asleep in the armchair opposite the formidable woman and her knitting needles.

His search took him to the dining hall, but it was bare, apart from the empty tables and chairs. Next, he knocked on Barry's door, but it appeared the bed hadn't even been touched the night before. Becoming increasingly worried, he went up to the next floor in search of Mathilda's room.

It was here he found Barry, sitting frozen and solemn on the edge of her bed. Robert's chest tightened, and he felt a little nauseous when he noticed that Mathilda wasn't there. Slowly he made his way to sit next to his friend. Not making a sound, Robert allowed just his presence to support Barry. What was there to say? No words are ever enough to console a person. Robert just wanted to ensure that Barry knew he wasn't alone, that he didn't have to be alone at a time like this.

Barry eventually broke the silence. "She went in her sleep."

"It was probably the best way," Robert comforted.

"I don't know if it was the best way." Barry wiped a tear from the glass of the picture frame in his hands. "I've spent every day of the last three years with her ghost … I've mourned her death so many times, even though physically she was here. I thought I had already shed all the tears I had to give for her … but … I'd give anything to have one more moment with her. Dementia or not … I never stopped loving her." Barry's body silently shook as more tears cascaded down his face.

Robert sympathetically placed a hand on his friend's shoulder. "We all knew how much you loved her, and I believe she never stopped loving you either." He reached over to the picture frame. "May I?"

Barry relinquished the photo with a small nod. Robert gently wiped the glass with his own handkerchief to remove any tearstains. The photo was of their wedding day, with Barry's espresso-dark skin and Mathilda's lighter cocoa bean shade clothed in white; the greyscale image depicted a wonderful day in amazing detail. Mathilda was a beautiful young woman, but her smile stood out in an essence of purity. Robert sighed at the fact that in his short time of knowing the couple, he had never seen her smile. Barry, himself a strapping young lad, looked so happy compared to his current self now sitting on the bed.

"She's beautiful," Barry mused to himself. "I came from Tobago when I was twenty-one. I first laid eyes on her the same day I arrived. It took me at least a week to find out who she was, but eventually, I found her. Even back then, she was always wearing those long flowery dresses like she still does … did … They were usually yellow, but she was such a colourful woman and always … always looked beautiful to me from the very depths of her soul."

"A woman worth loving when the beauty isn't skin deep," Robert added, subconsciously thinking back to his own failed marriage. He shook his head to escape from his forgotten thoughts.

"I became a postman, and Mathilda was a nurse. I swear, as soon as I could, I asked her to marry me." Barry smiled wistfully as Robert handed the picture back. "Honestly, life was hard, much harder than it ever had to be. But, through all the hard work and pain, we managed to raise two wonderful children, David and Mary. They have made their way in this harsh world and achieved so much more than either of us could have hoped for. David is an architect, and Mary works in property. She has tried to explain it to me, what it is exactly, but I never can remember. I'm just so proud of the both of them … and yet … I had to be the one to tell them she's gone."

"I'm sorry," Robert spoke quietly, unsure what else he could say to ease the pain.

"It's not your fault." Barry lifted his head and tried to smile for both of their sakes. "I don't think I can accept how cruel this world is or how little time I had with her. I selfishly believed we had eternity together … then, it was just me and her shadow … now she has been taken away from me completely … I don't think she knew I was even by her side."

"Barry, she knew, and at least her suffering has ended now."

"I know … I really do know, but … it's all so unfair in the grand scheme of things."

"Papa?" a woman's voice called from the doorway, breaking through the tears.

"Oh, my child," Barry cried out. Still clutching the photo in his arthritic hand, he almost ran into the arms of his daughter. They both held each other tightly, their tears free-flowing.

Robert stood up, trying not to disturb the reunion and made his way out of the room.

"Robert!" Barry called over his daughter's shoulder. "Thank you."

"Anytime, chap." Robert waved with a soft smile before he disappeared down the corridor.

Robert didn't know what to do with himself. He felt restless and agitated that he couldn't have been there for his friend earlier. It didn't take long for his heart to decide, and determinedly he grabbed his flute from his room and made his way into the garden.

It was never hard to find a quiet spot in the gardens of Mimosa Grange because not only were they vast, but also most of the residents didn't wish to leave the confines of the building they now called home. He made his way to the patio area directly out the back of the conservatory, then down the small flight of stone steps. Taking a sharp left, he went to the bench positioned against the wall in a recess where campanula grew as a waterfall backdrop.

Placing the case on the bench, he opened it and assembled his flute. With a quick run of his fingers to ensure the keys weren't sticky, he brought the flute to his mouth. The sound that flowed was enchanting in a mournful way. The melody was sorrowful, yet even the birds in the trees stopped to listen. Thankfully there was no wind to distort the sound, and high up on the second floor, Barry opened the window in his wife's room even more, leaning out with his daughter and son who had just joined them.

Robert thought of Romeo and Juliet, star-crossed lovers torn apart by a family feud, his own star-crossed lovers torn apart after so many years together by something as cruel as dementia. He remembered all the operas he had ever had the pleasure to be in the orchestra for, and equally, the tragedies that so many of the characters lamented over.

The result was a haunting sonata that told the story of his friend's heart-breaking love. It produced not only tears for Barry and his family but also tears that welled and tried to choke Robert as he let his heart play. The flute's ethereal sound penetrated to the very core of their souls.

AGED 85

After breakfast, Robert left the dining hall feeling once again grateful that he didn't need to worry about cooking or washing up. Though he missed his home and the freedom that granted, after two years, small pleasures could still be found in the little independence he had managed to keep here at Mimosa Grange.

One such pleasure was ambling her way towards him now. Dorothy Smalls was gorgeous in all respects. She was the oldest in the home, with a healthy age of ninety-seven. She was also the longest-running resident, and her familiarity with the building and everyone else within its walls was evidence of this. She walked the passageways almost by memory, taking the same routes every day. Yet despite her memory flaws and OCD tendencies, she was the kindest angel Robert had ever had the pleasure of knowing.

"Good morning, Dorothy," Robert smiled as she already held out an arm to stop him.

"Robert," she beamed. Then with a wink and holding her finger to her pursed lips in an effort to solicit secrecy, she shakily pulled out the crumpled white paper bag filled with chocolate limes. "Shh!"

He nodded in agreement and picked one of the wrapped boiled sweets out of the bag offered to him. With an exaggerated look around to see if anyone was watching, he winked in return and slipped the sweet into his cardigan pocket. All this extra suspicious detail was much to the benefit of Dorothy, who giggled like an adorable child as she patted his arm and then carried on making her way along behind her Zimmer frame.

Robert watched her small, hunched-over frame disappear before he continued in the opposite direction towards the Sun Lounge. Rounding the corner, he spotted Ashley bustling about in her trainers around one of the nurse's stations. Her athletic form and honey-coloured skin were a vast contrast to the wild, untamed ringlets that cascaded wildly around her head in a vivid purple.

"Purple looks good on you," Robert commented, catching her attention. "Much better than the green you had last time."

"Thank you, Robert." Ashley grinned before adding in a serious tone, "I swear, I'm not letting my sister and green hair dye in the same room ever again!"

"Well, in any case, it's admirable that you help your sister out in her hairdressing career." Robert tried to stifle his laughter as he thought back to the garish green she was sporting unwillingly until last week.

"It's all for your amusement," she quipped back before laughing with him.

Robert slipped a hand into his pocket and pulled out the chocolate lime. With a quick mischievous glance, he held it up against her hair, resulting in squeals of breathless laughter from Ashley before she pocketed the sweet in her uniform. He gave her a wink and continued on his route to the Sun Lounge.

He was usually one of the first to finish breakfast, and it had now become routine that he would prepare a seat and crossword, ready for when John could join him. Over the past year, Barry had joined them more often, too. He had declined his family's wishes to move him out of Mimosa Grange after Mathilda's death.

Paper ready before him and pen secured in his breast pocket, he sat back and crossed his legs, one over the other, hands folded in his lap. He let his thoughts wander to Dorothy Smalls: her wrinkled face showing the years of laughter and always a constant reminder of her kindness of character. That and her penchant for chocolate limes. Robert chuckled to himself as he continued to reminisce.

His first meeting with Dorothy was when she accosted him for a chocolate lime. Mike, who was showing Robert around at the time, had even commented that he didn't think he had 'ever seen her smile so much.' Robert had felt that she had singled him out for a reason and not just because he was a new face. His suspicions were confirmed about six months later.

It so happened that Robert's curiosity had grown the better of him. Dorothy never received visitors, and he was intrigued about where her never-ending supply of chocolate limes came from. So, one rainy day after the daily sweet offering had happened, he followed her on one of the shuffling routes she took back to her room. He watched from the doorway as she opened the bedside cabinet, pulled out another paper bag and proceeded to select a new chocolate lime to replace the one Robert had taken from the usual worn bag that resided in her pocket.

"Robert?" Ashley's voice questioned from behind him.

"Good God!" Robert jumped back, holding a hand to his beating heart.

"I'm so sorry!" Ashley held out her hands frantically as if to catch him.

"I'm not so decrepit to have a heart attack; calm down," he joked. "Mind you, you did give me a start."

Ashley dropped her arms, relaxing. "And what are you doing?"

"Well," he glanced quickly into Dorothy's room before gently motioning Ashley to follow him, "I was curious about the limes."

"Limes?"

"Yes, the chocolate limes she always offers me."

"Ah, I see … that's a long story."

"I have the rest of my life to hear it," Robert winked.

Ashley rolled her eyes, then beckoned with a hand that he follow her away from Dorothy's earshot. "You've noticed that she doesn't receive visitors?"

"Indeed, I have."

"Dorothy told me a lot when she first moved in, though I doubt she remembers at all anymore. She is a twenties baby, and she had a younger brother. They had childhood memories of their father bringing home chocolate limes for them to share. Then they were caught up in the midst of war, and their father was, unfortunately, a casualty of the Blitz. After the war, it was her brother who one day bought some chocolate limes for the two of them.

"She described it with such fondness, despite the hardships the family had faced. I really believe that chocolate limes became a symbol of better times for them. In any case, whatever happened in her life gets a bit hazy until just up to before she came here. She never had children, and she never mentioned a husband. Her brother didn't have a family either, so the two lived together."

Ashley paused, and Robert noticed her eyes had lost their usual sparkle. She took a deep breath before continuing. "I remember the day her brother turned up to look at the place."

"What happened?" Robert spoke softly, fearing the worst for this conversation.

"He decided this was the home where he wanted his sister to spend the rest of her days. I believe the last years of their living together had highlighted the condition of her mind, and he had almost become a carer for her.

"He was diagnosed with mesothelioma: cancer from asbestos. He was given a year, and he declined some medical help so that he didn't prolong his suffering … Actually, I believe all his motives were genuinely fuelled by his care and concern for his sister. He left her here with us with a note stating where he was going to be buried. I don't think he could bring himself to explain to her why, and if he ever did, she never showed us reasons to believe she understood. Their farewell was fond and unforgettable. The last thing he did was give her a white paper bag of chocolate limes, kiss her forehead, and tell her not to wait up for him." Ashley wiped away a small tear that had escaped and blinked away the others.

Robert stood solemnly next to her, unsure of what to say next.

Ashley broke the silence. "She's taken quite a fancy to you, though."

"Do I share a name with her brother?"

"No, his name was Alan. To be honest, you don't look alike at all … though … there's something about your eyes …"

Robert stared at her a little longer before turning away to gaze out the window. He felt a weight of responsibility beginning to encompass him as he comprehended his role in Dorothy's world. The white paper bag she continued to use to carry her offerings around in her pocket was lovingly kept, wrinkled, slightly torn and just as important to her as the sweets themselves.

"It's not the same paper bag with the original chocolate limes from her brother?" Robert asked in a moment of sickening horror as he recounted all the times he had taken one of the offered sweets. One hand reflexively rested on his stomach as the other covered his mouth.

"Oh no! You didn't think …" Ashley burst out laughing. "We restock them as and when we notice her stash is running low. New paper bags as well; we're lucky that there's an old-fashioned sweet shop in the middle of town. Though it's hardly a problem, I think chocolate limes are one of the few sweets they haven't discontinued yet."

"Oh, thank goodness!" Robert sighed, his hands relaxing.

"Imagine what you would have done if I said they were the originals!"

"Oh, please, my dear. I've had enough scares from you for one day!"

"I'm sorry," Ashley bit her lip to muffle her giggling.

"Ashley, could you help me?" he began thoughtfully.

"Sure thing, Rob." She looked at him quizzically.

"I'd like to get some more chocolate limes. They're precious to her, after all. Then every time she offers me one, I'll pass it back to you, and you can return it to her stash. She'll truly have a never-ending supply that way. Besides, what's left of my own teeth won't last much longer if I keep eating boiled sweets."

Ashley agreed readily, and their plan had remained in action up until today.

Robert slowly brought himself out of his reverie as Barry came in, pushing John in his wheelchair. The three deliberated over the daily crossword together until it was mentioned that Robert seemed unfocused.

"Sorry, I've been thinking," Robert mused.

"About what?" Barry seemed intrigued, even if John was perturbed by the pausing of their intellectual pastime.

"Dorothy," Robert turned to them, a fire in his eyes. "What if we played a game tonight?"

"What do you mean by game?" John questioned with a glance over the top of his glasses.

"Well, what if we all share the chocolate limes together?"

"Chocolate limes?"

"Yes, they really are important to her, and I want to help make a new memory for her with all of us." He turned to look at Barbara from her throne in the corner, brandishing her knitting needles. "You will join in too, won't you, Babs?"

"I will do no such thing over a boiled sweet!" she muttered disdainfully.

"Not even for a glass of whisky?" Robert sweetly coaxed.

Barbara's needles froze, and her eyes flickered as she processed the bribe dangled before her. "As long as it's just one sweet." She gave a resolute huff, and the clicking of her knitting needles resumed again.

"It sounds a lark," Barry beamed excitedly.

"It sounds ridiculous," John added. "Count me in, all the same."

"That's settled then," Robert rubbed his hands together in anticipation. "This evening after dinner. I'll start it off."

"Why do I get the feeling you are used to starting antics off?" Barbara commented to herself.

That evening, the five of them were sitting in the Sun Lounge. Despite the number of seats available, they had endeavoured to be in a circle around one of the coffee tables, much to Barbara's annoyance at having been uprooted from her usual armchair.

Robert purposely placed himself next to the oblivious Dorothy. He had forewarned Ashley, who was still on shift, of their plan and asked her to ignore them completely. Then, a little while after they had settled themselves, Robert gently nudged Dorothy's arm to catch her attention. She looked at him adoringly. Robert winked at her and produced a small neat white paper bag of his own from his cardigan pocket, offering her a chocolate lime.

Dorothy's face lit up in an explosion of love, and she shakily took one of the sweets, all the while giggling like a little child. She carefully unwrapped the green sweet and popped it into her mouth, savouring the taste with closed eyes.

Robert couldn't help the large grin on his face; her smile of pure, innocent enjoyment was infectious. He waited until Dorothy was looking at him again before he over-exaggeratedly looked to see who was watching before offering the bag to John, who was sitting in his wheelchair next to him.

Dorothy clung to Robert's arm with great enthusiasm. Little squeaks of excitement escaped from her as she squeezed his arm each time she watched the sweet bag pass around to the next person.

Barry, who was sitting opposite her, took great delight in making faces at her. Now and then, he looked around to check the carers weren't watching before sticking his tongue and a half-sucked chocolate lime out. It was all much to the amusement of Dorothy, who laughed gaily, never letting go of Robert as she enjoyed the spectacle before her.

Even Barbara showed off the sweet in her hand with an appreciative nod towards Dorothy, though her eyes were on Robert and her thoughts on the tot of whisky she would be enjoying later.

Ashley jumped in once or twice with her acting skills, looking at the group suspiciously with a raised eyebrow before carrying on with her duties. In all honesty, her heart was melting at the pure soul Dorothy possessed and the lengths Robert was willing to go to make her smile. She couldn't wait to tell the other staff, especially Jessica who was working in the kitchen.

The evening passed with great merriment. Robert himself was even beginning to feel at home with his unconventional family, though his home life had never been like this. Even though he dared not believe it himself, he liked to think he had, just on this one occasion, been worthy of the admiration Dorothy bestowed upon him.

CHAPTER 5

AGED 86

Images flooded the dark canvas of his eyelids, intermingling with the early morning sun spots that dotted his skin in a warming glow. A sweet blonde-haired child that ran into his arms after he came home from work. The tired eyes that sadly smiled at him as the door shut between them for the last time. The cries of broken hearts begging for a family life that fell apart before he could even breathe. The mistakes that changed his music for better or for worse, and the loneliness that consumed him.

The soft click of the record player's needle prompted Robert out of his armchair. Methodically, he replaced the record with another, carefully brushing it clean of dust before replacing the needle. He returned to his chair, closing his eyes and tapping the time with his finger as he let the music take over, once again escaping his own thoughts. It wasn't the first time he had thought of his past and questioned his circumstances, and he was sure it wouldn't be the last, but he had long since given up looking for the answers.

A knock at the door prompted him to open his eyes again. "Yes? Come in."

"Robert?"

"Martin! Come in, come in. How are you?" Robert beckoned joyfully for his friend and beloved apprentice for many years within the music industry to enter and take a seat as he began to raise himself from his chair.

Martin motioned for him to stay where he was and, after hauling a large box into the corner of the room, perched himself down on the bed opposite him.

"Your chess table as per our agreement," Martin huffed, a little red-faced, though he was still beaming from ear to ear. "Nice place you've got here."

"Thank you." Robert glanced over to the box in the corner with a wistful smile before turning his attention back to his friend. "I thought you were still in Sweden."

"Got back yesterday morning, booked a hotel down the road from here, and you're top of my list this morning."

"It's been a while since I last saw you."

"Nearly four years," Martin replied sullenly. "I'm sorry it's taken me so long. Work got in the way massively."

"It usually does for us."

"Not to fear, I got all your letters, and your manuscripts are big sellers. You're partly to blame; you've helped keep me busy."

"My apologies," Robert chuckled. "It's so good to see you, old friend. You look like you've put weight on," Robert remarked before jokingly adding, "the high life treating you well then?"

"Well, it was until the American incident, and don't get me started with the communication confusion in Denmark before I even got to Sweden."

"You need to stop being so good at your job; then they wouldn't summon you to sort these things out."

"True, but it pays well. Besides, I wouldn't be able to be the forerunner for your music if I gave up work. Speaking of which ..." Martin pulled out a folded envelope from his inside jacket pocket. "Your last letter seemed rather urgent. That can't be just because of your beloved chess board, hm?"

Robert shook his head slightly before taking a deep breath. "I want you to be the executor of my will."

"What? Now look here, chap, I know you're in this godforsaken place, but that doesn't mean it's the end yet. Does it?" Martin's eyes widened in concern.

"Being here has opened my eyes to many things, one of which is this isn't a godforsaken place." He glanced at his friend before continuing. "Secondly, no one lives forever. Now, don't look at me like that. I'm in perfect health for the moment, but remember, I have nearly twenty years on you."

Martin sighed and nodded in admission of the facts laid before him. "I would be honoured to help you in any way I can, especially as executor of your will. But don't take that as permission to kick the bucket as soon as my name is printed on paper." He waggled a warning finger at him.

Chuckling, Robert eased himself out of his chair and made his way to the box in the corner, shakily beginning to attack the confines of the tape. Martin rose and helped to uncover the prized possession of the chess table. Once it was free of all the cardboard and bubble wrap, Robert caressed the wood slowly and delicately until his hand happened across the drawer that the pieces were stored in, pulling them out and gently placing them on the board haphazardly. Martin continued to watch in a bemused manner. Finally, with all the pieces out of the way, Robert pushed down on the bottom of the drawer with a soft click. Slowly lifting the panel, he retrieved the parchment stored there.

"You're kidding me!" Martin gasped as he fumbled behind him for support. Eventually, he found the bed and collapsed down, his eyes still fixed on Robert's hand and the parchment he was now unfolding. "Don't tell me I had it all this time?"

"I may not have been a good father, but I knew my daughter well enough to prepare." Robert's voice trembled as he stood, shakily reading his previously written will. With a deep breath, he removed a lighter from his bedside cabinet and lit a corner of the parchment. Then, making his way into the bathroom, he held it until the flames consumed the majority before he proceeded to drop it into the shower.

Martin stared in disbelief, his brain twisting in each direction as it pieced together the events of the last few moments.

"I'll call my solicitor and have a new will drafted and sent to you directly for signing," Robert remarked as he exited the bathroom.

"I'm assuming that the now non-existent will referred to Lisa?"

"Indeed. I didn't have much time to prepare before coming here, and I suppose I was still hoping that she would find a conscience. So, in my attempt to prevent her from seeing the will and getting any ideas, I hid it in the chess table before sending it to you for safekeeping. I'm sorry I didn't tell you."

Martin pondered to himself for a moment before replying. "This whole affair leaves a bad taste in my mouth. Don't get me wrong," he added hurriedly, "I find no fault in what you're doing. But I feel as though your hand has been forced, and I cannot for the life of me fathom why."

"I don't think there's ever just one answer for why. In any case, this is the path Lisa has chosen for us. It doesn't mean I won't fight it in my own way. It's been like this for over four years, and my hope for her to change will never go away; however, I won't facilitate this any more than I did then."

Martin nodded in thoughtful agreement. "Hang on, why didn't the smoke alarm go off when you burnt the will?" His eyes narrowed in suspicion.

"I may be old, but I'm not deaf. The bloody thing needed new batteries and was constantly beeping. So, I stood on the chair and took the batteries out."

"Robert!"

"Now, hear me out; that was only last night. I was waiting to see Mike today, and I was going to ask him for some new batteries. Mike's the chap that I ask to send letters for me."

"You are still mischief wrapped up in a musician's attire." Martin rolled his eyes.

"Talking of Mike," Robert added, "he has a daughter called Amiyah who plays flute too. He shows me videos on that … mobile gadget of his quite often."

"Now, I'm assuming you're telling me this not as a prideful old man who's bored of his care home but because you truly believe she has talent." Martin winked with a large grin.

"Of course!" Robert felt almost indignant.

"Need I remind you that you're retired?" Martin joked.

"Hardly!" Robert scoffed before raising an eyebrow at his protégé. "You'll consider her in the future, Marty, if she truly does wish to go professional?"

"Of course. I've never doubted your judgment before; I'm not going to start now."

"That's my boy!" Robert fondly patted him on the back.

Catching a glance at his watch, Martin suddenly stood up, "I'm sorry to cut things short, Rob. I've got a meeting in half an hour. I'll try not to be such a stranger from now on. Keep up the good work and run Mike off his feet, sending the letters and manuscripts to me."

"And I'll get on to the solicitors later today." He caught Martin's outstretched hand and grasped it firmly. "Thank you for everything you do, Marty."

"Anything for a good boss!" Martin winked. With a final squeeze of his hand, they released their grip, and he left, an amused grin still plastered to his face.

CHAPTER 6

AGED 87

S at among the bushes at the bottom of the main garden steps, Robert's breath sailed effortlessly, becoming pure notes of melody. His eyes closed as he let his heart direct his fingers, his foot lightly tapping the beat to follow.

When the music stopped, he paused momentarily, soaking in the atmosphere of the quiet surroundings. The birds were chirping; their evening songs intermingled with the faint voices from Mimosa Grange behind him, the top note played by a pair of court shoes clicking their way across the flagstone path.

He opened his eyes and looked down at his flute case beside him. With a small sigh, he began to dismantle his flute and clean each piece meticulously.

"Mr Sallow?" an authoritative voice questioned as the court heels came down the steps.

"I'm here, Ms Doherty," he replied without looking up.

"Mr Sallow, do you know how long I've been looking for you?"

"Not very long, I'm sure." Robert smiled to himself.

Amanda inhaled sharply before sitting down on the bench next to him. "Well, that's as may be … but I can't keep having residents not showing up for dinner."

"Ah, Mandy, I have a solution to that."

"Rob, unless it requires you in the dining hall for meals with the other residents …" She raised an eyebrow in a curious sideways glance that encouraged him to continue.

"Well, the way I see it, it's been so hot these days that I haven't been able to come into the garden for my flute practice. Now, I don't think any of us want me to practice the same pieces continuously in my room, perhaps with mistakes … no one likes music when it's played wrong. And I really can't bear to miss a day's practice. Hence with enough daylight and warmth still left outside, I need to practice at the optimal time, which just so happens to coincide with dinner.

With his flute clean and placed gently back in its case, he shut the lid and lifted his eyes to meet hers. "We need a summerhouse."

"A … summerhouse?"

"Yes. It has occurred to me today that the garden has no shelter from the elements."

"It's a lovely idea, Rob …" Amanda sighed, "but there's no way we could ever get the money for such a project."

Robert dropped his head. "I know that's the case, Mandy. But I felt I had to say my piece."

"I'm glad you did."

"To set the record straight, I'm not trying to be facetious and force my point across. I genuinely prefer this temperature to practice. It is way too hot during the day. I don't mind missing a meal or two."

"Try five. I've had nearly a whole week of you missing dinner." Amanda smiled at him. "I won't ask you to stop your flute practice; it's a part of who you are, but I can't have you skipping out on any more meal times."

"Can I not have meals in my room afterwards?"

"You know I can't allow that legally. Besides, if I do it for you, I have to do it for all the residents."

"Summerhouse?"

"Don't push it!" Amanda chuckled, gently nudging his arm. "How about we try you practising in the function hall at a more reasonable time that doesn't affect meal times?"

"Only if you promise to at least consider a summerhouse for the wellbeing of the residents." Robert winked at her as he stood up.

Amanda shook her head with a soft smile before agreeing. Raising herself to stand next to him, she held out her hand. "Deal!"

They made their way back inside, where the evening warmth was briefly interrupted by an icy chill as they acclimatised to the air conditioning.

Robert bid his farewells for the evening as they parted ways; Amanda returned to her office whilst he made his way back towards his room. The heat of the day had yet again been exhausting, and though the building itself was vastly cooler, the climb up the stairs was slow.

Nearing his room, he noticed the lights were on and his door open. Cautiously he peered around the doorframe to see the slender, muscular frame of Ashley before him, her hair a myriad of waterfall blues.

"I don't do private concerts, I'm afraid," he remarked loudly as he neared the desk to place down his flute.

"Holy mother-"

"Ah!" Robert cautioned her with a stern finger as he winked. "What pleasure brings you to my room this evening?"

"Robert Sallow!" Ashley rebuked. "You scared me out of my wits! Were you always this much trouble? No, don't answer that; I'm pretty sure you were. In any case, I brought you something to nibble."

Robert smiled cheekily at her before glancing at the desk behind them. Upon it, carefully wrapped in clingfilm, were a few sandwiches and a packet of crisps. He brought his attention back to her. "You didn't need to go to the trouble."

"I know," she smiled almost shyly. "I didn't see you in the dinner hall. So, I went to look for you. I'd just made it outside, where I could hear your music, when Amanda stopped me and told me not to bother you. She said it was because of the hot weather and that she would have a talk with you."

"I didn't mean to worry you." Robert patted her arm gently.

"So, when I went back to the kitchen at the end of dinner, I spoke to Jess. She prepared this for you; we didn't want you to go hungry. We can't give you leftover hot food."

"Ashley, it's fine; you don't need to explain to me. Thank you very much for thinking of me, both of you!" Robert sat down in his armchair with a sigh. "I'm a lucky man to have food angels deliver to my room."

"We're not making a habit of it, you hear?" Ashley warned lightly with a smile.

"Yes, Ma'am," Robert saluted mockingly. "And how is your dear wife in the kitchen?"

"Jess is very well, thank you. We're looking into buying our first home together instead of just renting the dingy flat we currently have."

"Well, that's a big move. Are you hoping to start a family later too?"

"We haven't considered that yet … not really anyway …" Ashley began picking at her nails as she looked down towards her feet. "Besides, it's not that easy for us."

"No one ever said it would be easy," Robert remarked kindly, "but it's not impossible. Especially in this day and age."

"Thank you for being so supportive," she blurted out in a rush of emotion before blushing at her outburst.

"Silly child! I know my generation are a load of grumpy old farts who are sticklers for 'the good old days,' but it doesn't mean people aren't free to love. Look at history; you most certainly are not the first female couple, and I can guarantee you will not be the last either."

"But …"

"But people will always voice their disdain to everyone and their praise to a select few. Ignore the hate of this world; such a lovely couple should be granted happiness and luck."

"I'm starting to think you are not just trouble but a sweet talker too!"

"Tongue coated in honey, as my mother used to say." Robert chuckled.

CHAPTER 7

AGED 88

Winter was particularly harsh this year. Robert sat on the end of his bed, staring at his bare feet. He had tried several times to put his socks on, but his stomach pitched and his head tormented him every time he attempted.

"Rob?" Mike's voice called softly from the doorway. "You alright?"

"I'm … fine," Robert pulled a wistful smile as he tried to look up at Mike. "There's another letter on the sideboard …"

"Let me help you." Mike crouched down in front of him and gently held his hand out for the socks still clamped in Robert's shaky hand.

Reluctantly releasing his grip, he let the fabric fall into Mike's hand as his heart dropped with sickening fear. He squeezed his eyes closed, forcing any threatening tears away as Mike deftly pulled on his socks and shoes.

"Thank you," Robert choked, unable to look him in the eyes. "I can manage now."

Mike placed a hand on his shoulder and patted it gently a couple of times before leaving without saying a word, picking up the letter as he left.

Robert breathed out low and slowly. His cheeks felt flushed with the embarrassment that bubbled away deep within him. Blinking his eyes open to banish any remnants of tears, he gave another deep breath and steeled himself to rise.

With an inaudible groan, he stood, wobbling as he regained his balance. Setting his sights on the doorway, he paced his way carefully.

Once moving, his stomach seemed to settle, and his head cleared. Pushing all thoughts of the morning's embarrassment away completely, he focused on his usual routine.

❀ ❀ ❀

Barry and John both eyed him carefully over breakfast. Robert tried to ease their concerns by laughing it off, though neither seemed relieved in the slightest. He changed the topic completely, bringing to the forefront the excitement and importance of today.

"Dorothy is finally a century-year-old!" He glanced at each of them in turn before returning his focus to the half-eaten bland toast before him. "I wonder if she's received her telegram from The Queen yet?" His face visibly uncomfortable, Robert pushed the remainder of his breakfast to one side, nausea gripping his stomach as he contemplated trying to eat more.

"I can't imagine living for that long," Barry remarked absently.

"Och, Laddie, you're not as young as you like to think!" John quipped with a hearty laugh.

"Just make sure to live long enough to see me get my telegram!"

"Christ! You think Queenie will live that long?"

"Well, not much point living to one hundred then; if I don't get my congratulations."

"I met her once," Robert interjected quietly, still staring at his now cold breakfast.

Barry and John turned to face him slowly, their hands dropping from where they had been clapping each other on the back.

Barry swallowed audibly before speaking. "Why don't you rest in your room today? Maybe you're coming down with a cold, what with still practising your flute outside until recently?"

"No, no … I'm fine," Robert smiled weakly at them. "Just thinking about playing for Dorothy's birthday, that's all. Always get a little nervous playing in front of people, even at my age. I'll go and get the crossword ready for us. I'll see you chaps in a bit."

Robert pushed back his chair and tried to hide the fact that he used the table to support himself for a little longer than usual as he stood up. With a final regretful glance at his breakfast, he sighed and shuffled out of the dining hall. His companions watched glumly as he disappeared.

With his eyes shut, Robert tried his best to relax into his chair in the Sun Lounge. His thoughts circulated in worrying ruminations as his own realisations of his current frailty surfaced. He had rather hoped that bland toast would have quietened his stomach, though the dizziness told him that wish was futile.

Mustering his strength, he focused on his breathing, long and slow, steadying his pace as much as he could. He was pulling out all the stops to appear his normal, relatively healthy self before his friends. He wasn't holding out much confidence on its efficacy, deciding instead, as Barry wheeled John into the room, that he would push the nausea to one side and ignore it as best he could.

The crossword was proving to be a challenge for the three of them combined, so it was a welcome break when Julia arrived with young Samuel. Not long afterwards, Mary and David both showed up to spend time with Barry. Gratefully, Robert made his excuses and headed back to his room, rejecting the persuasions from all the visitors for him to stay.

In the corridor, outside his room, he met with Ashley, bustling around in her trainers and sporting a fiery colour combination of ringlets tied loosely on top of her head.

"Good morning, Rob," she called cheerfully before pausing and raising an eyebrow at him. "You alright there, troublemaker?"

"Just thought I'd have some time alone; all the families have come to visit … I don't want to be an extra wheel," Robert tried to smile as he entered his room.

"You sure that's all?" Ashley asked gently as she leaned through the doorway.

"Quite sure." Robert lifted the lid on his record player and proceeded to dust off a record before lowering the needle and then himself into his armchair. "I'll take the time to reacquaint myself with Mozart before returning to the fray."

"Just call if you need anything," Ashley replied as she watched him close his eyes.

He lifted a hand in acknowledgement before succumbing to his musical reverie.

The afternoon winter sun lazily lit up the room and gently warmed his face. Slowly blinking his eyes open, he took a moment to come round and fully realise where he was. Looking down, he saw a blanket tucked around his legs. Glancing over to the record player, he noticed the needle was lifted. His eyes found the alarm clock stationed next to it. Stretching carefully, he raised his hands and wiped them over his face with an exhausted sigh. Moving the blanket to one side, he put all his energy into standing up. His stomach didn't betray him though his head threatened to spin again. With a couple of deep breaths, he steeled himself, collected his flute and the small little package wrapped neatly beside it and made his way downstairs.

Halfway up the stairs, Mike was heading in the opposite direction.

"You're awake! Feeling any better? I did come and check on you a couple of times. Oh, and I stopped the record player too. Amiyah told me that's what I should do; I could hear her voice telling me off if I had just left it." He ran an embarrassed hand across the back of his head.

"Thank you, I really appreciate it, and for the blanket," Robert replied.

"Ah, no problem. I was actually just coming your way to wake you up. Didn't think you'd want to miss Dorothy's birthday dinner."

"Indeed, I don't! It's not every day someone you know turns one hundred."

"Of course. I'm just going for the cake, but don't tell anyone." Mike winked before running another hand behind his head in bashful laughter.

Together the two of them made their way down the rest of the stairs, heading for the dining hall. Dorothy was already sitting at the head of one of the tables; a paper party hat in neon colours sat precariously on top of her soft white curls. Her eyes were wide, and a smile graced her face, but her pure happiness didn't sparkle in her eyes until her gaze fell on Robert as he made his way over to her.

"Happy birthday, my dear Dorothy," he smiled fondly at her as she mouthed his name in greeting. He carefully placed the small gift he had brought with him into her outstretched hand.

In surprised confusion, she placed it squarely in front of her before reaching her hand to squeeze his arm as had become their customary greeting along with the chocolate limes. Struggling to take her eyes off him, she retracted her hand and methodically and precisely unwrapped her present, folding the ribbon and paper neatly and placing it to one side as she did so.

Eventually, she revealed a piece of silky fabric, its marbled navy blues and pearlescent whites stretching into an eloquent scarf. A squeak of excitement left her lips as she shakily held a hand in front of her mouth. With her eyes flickering fast to fall on Robert's face again, she caught his hand in a tight grip of gleeful devotion.

Robert gave her hand a loving squeeze back before picking up the scarf to drape it around her shoulders, the colours highlighting her usual pearls that hung around her neck. She looked down, mesmerised at the fabric as it shimmered, gently flowing from her shoulders. Robert let the end of the scarf drop from his hand. Catching Dorothy's attention, he rummaged in his cardigan pocket and revealed a solitary chocolate lime that he proudly placed in her hands. Her infectious giggling filled the room.

"Oh, that's beautiful!" Ashley exclaimed as she came over to check on the both of them. Dorothy beamed back before returning her gaze to Robert as he pulled back the chair next to her to sit down.

Barry and John were already sitting around at the table, putting on a show of winking at Robert in overly-masculine banter, not only through their enjoyment of making a point of Dorothy's fondness for him but also to help distract them all from the events of the morning.

Barbara dominated the other end of the table, becoming rather frustrated at Ashley and Mike's response of 'no whisky.' "What kind of party celebration doesn't have alcohol? She's one hundred, for goodness' sake! It's an outrage!"

The birthday dinner hadn't changed much from the usual menu, though homecooked fish and chips still tasted better somehow in the knowledge of today's importance. After the plates were cleared away, Jessica arrived from the kitchen brandishing a large tray, the contents of which were covered with a cloth.

Robert found himself smiling at the thought of how different Ashley was from her wife. Though Jessica's hair was dyed a fantastic deep shade of iris purple, no doubt another creation from Ashley's younger sister, her plump figure and marshmallow skin made them as different as chalk and cheese.

"What are you smiling to yourself for, troublemaker?" Ashley joked as she tapped him on the shoulder. "Good job with the scarf, by the way."

"Well, it's all thanks to you helping me with that device you call a phone," Robert remarked matter-of-factly.

"Well, now that you mention it, I suppose we're even after your contribution to the cake design." Ashley grinned cheekily as she went to help Jessica remove the cloth to reveal a mass of chocolate cupcakes.

Amanda had joined the fray of residents who were eagerly awaiting a piece of cake as Mike turned off the lights. A single flame flickered in the darkened room from Jessica's hand as she lit the solitary candle on top of the many cupcakes she had brought in. The room erupted into a wobbly rendition of Happy Birthday as the cupcake in question was brought before Dorothy. The flame reflected off the chocolate lime cemented in the chocolate icing like a fiery emerald being presented to its queen—a queen who gracefully and effortlessly blew out the candle.

The lights flickered back on, and the staff began bustling about, handing out the delicious morsels to everyone in the room. Amanda caught Robert's attention and gave a brief nod with a gesture of encouragement. Nodding back, he brought his flute case out from under the table and proceeded to assemble it. Taking a deep breath, he raised himself from the table and made his way to stand closer to the centre of the room where everyone could get a better chance of hearing him.

Barry and John exchanged worried glances; nevertheless, they watched after him with encouragement. Ashley and Jessica were standing next to each other, watching eagerly, though Robert could sense their worry too. Mike nodded his head reassuringly as he stood behind Dorothy. Finally, Robert's eyes focused on Dorothy's face. Her twinkling eyes never tore themselves away from him, her hands absentmindedly twirling the ends of the scarf around her fingers, and she smiled softly as she sucked eagerly at the chocolate lime he had presented earlier.

Robert smiled in return as he brought the flute up to his lips. He had worked tirelessly on his composition for the last couple of months. Even though it was the traditional Happy Birthday tune, he had embellished it with all the memories that he and his dear Dorothy shared. It was a congratulatory piece that celebrated her life. It was Dorothy's life condensed into a hauntingly beautiful soundtrack that evoked tears and placed smiles on listeners' faces. It showcased her cheeky childish side whilst maintaining her eloquence of soft-spoken womanly manner. She was an angel placed centrally and solely in his symphony.

His fingers flowed over the keys as naturally as second nature would allow, due to his hours of practice. His breath, usually controlled and precise, began to falter. He squinted in twisted concentration as he pursued the next note, then the next. He couldn't stop now! His chest tightened as the pit of his stomach dropped. The sea of darkness claimed his body as he succumbed to the waves of nausea and dizziness.

A tear escaped to fall from his face as he saw Dorothy scream inaudibly as she tried to push herself away from the table to get to him, being held back by Barry. Mike was already running towards him along with Ashley and Jessica.

In his world of darkness, the authoritative voice of Amanda issuing commands, the evacuation of the residents to another room, and the subsequent phone call to the ambulance, filled his ears.

A voice called softly in his ear repeatedly. His hand was warm despite how cold the rest of him felt; another shiver shook his body. He opened his eyes slowly, dreading what or who he would see.

Mike was standing at the side of the bed, gently consoling a distraught Dorothy, who clutched Robert's hand in her own. She was sitting on the edge of the armchair, attempting to get as close as she could to her dear friend. Her eyes were red from crying, and she kept sniffing as she nodded in acknowledgement of Mike's words.

"My Dorothy …" Robert's voice cracked as he tried to raise his hand to wipe away her stray tears.

"Robert!" she burst into a flood of broken sobs as she clutched at his hand even tighter, shaking in a mixture of shock, relief, and frailty.

"Welcome back, Rob," Mike smiled with sad eyes. "How are you feeling?"

"Rough …"

"I'm not surprised. You gave us a scare back there, all of us."

"I'm sorry."

"Now, don't start that! We're here to help you. Let us do that much, at least. I'm going to get Amanda; she's just outside talking to Dr Prior."

Robert watched as Mike disappeared through the doorway though his voice was still clearly heard. He gave a deep sigh as his eyes dropped back to Dorothy.

"I'm sorry, my dear."

"You shouldn't have pushed yourself so hard for me." Her delicate voice wavered as she held back another wave of tears.

"Of course I should," Robert smiled at her exhaustedly. "You made the century! How could I not celebrate that with you?"

"But it's my fault you're ill … You're here because of me."

"Not at all! Don't be silly, my dear. I'm sorry I ruined your birthday!"

He swallowed with a wince of pain as he tried to sit up, causing Dorothy to become flustered. He compromised by lying back down again and weakly squeezing her hand comfortingly.

"Robert?" Amanda's voice caught their attention. "How are you feeling?"

"I've been better," he sighed, raising his unoccupied hand to his forehead. "I'm sorry for all the fuss."

"Well, never mind, we just need to focus on getting you better now. You have a few bruises but nothing too serious. Dr Prior will be in again in a short while to discuss with you how we proceed going forward. You must tell any of us if you don't feel well in the slightest. Shelve the independence for a few days while we get you back up to scratch."

"Yes, Ma'am!"

Amanda shook her head with a soft smile as she disappeared from view.

"Do you have a chocolate lime?" he asked quietly, a hint of a cheeky smile on his lips.

Dorothy nodded and released his hand momentarily to fish out the crumpled paper bag from her pocket, offering the contents to him. He took one gratefully, rolling the boiled sugar around his mouth with his tongue. Dorothy resuming to hold his hand between both of hers, stroking it absently with her thumbs whilst staring at his face. He smiled at her lovingly as he closed his eyes in an attempt to process all that had happened.

"My flute!" He bolted up straight in his exclamation, startling Dorothy before the dizziness rushed in a flow of blood to the brain. He lay back down rather hurriedly, trying not to choke on the chocolate lime in his mouth.

"Where's my flute?" he asked aloud again, though a lot calmer.

"I have it," Mike interrupted as he re-entered the room, checking on Dorothy before he continued. "I'll take it home to Amiyah to have it checked over; it took quite the fall with you. Besides, you don't need any encouragement to play at the moment. You just need to rest."

"If little Amiyah is involved, then I know it is in safe hands," he sighed. "Thank you."

"No problem. Now get some rest."

Robert nodded slowly, fatigue washing over him once more. Mike pushed the armchair a little closer and helped Dorothy shuffle backwards into the cushions before draping a blanket over her knees. She squeezed his arm briefly in thanks before focusing her attention on Robert's hand in hers once more, her eyes struggling to stay open as her thumbs stroked the back of his. Robert turned his head to face her with a weak smile. He could never express how grateful he was for her presence right now. He had dreaded becoming old and decrepit, not for the aches and pains but for the loneliness. And yet, Dorothy was the angel he felt he didn't deserve.

"Thank you, my dear." He squeezed her hand briefly before falling back to sleep.

CHAPTER 8

AGED 89

66 Hello?" Robert took the phone from Amanda and waved in thanks as she retreated back to her office. "Robert Sallow speaking." He winced slightly as he settled down in the office chair behind the front desk.

"Rob, it's me."

"Marty! How you doing, my boy?"

"Not bad, not bad. Just got back from Japan in the early hours of this morning; thought I'd check up on you before I catch up on my sleep."

"Still overworking then, I see," Robert chuckled. "How was Japan?"

"They are loving your last composition; I don't suppose you fancy a trip away from the home?"

"Now then, we've discussed this. In my current state, if it's not a day trip to where I can come home whenever I feel I need to, then I won't be going anywhere anytime soon."

"You're acting your age, for once. I'm almost disappointed." Martin sighed dramatically, followed by a low laugh. "I understand, Rob. You have to do what's best for you."

"Thank you, Marty, for everything."

"Now, don't go getting sentimental on me. You've got years left in you yet!"

"Alright, alright, enough about this." Robert waved the topic aside. "You need to catch up with your sleep before your next travels!"

"Indeed, that I do."

"It was good to hear your voice, Marty." Robert blinked back his watery eyes.

"Anytime, old chap."

The soft click of the call disconnecting prompted Robert to reluctantly return the phone back to its station. He stared for a while, almost hoping it would ring again. With a sigh, he tapped his walking stick firmly on the floor and eased himself up out of the chair. He took a few doddery steps as he straightened himself and found his balance.

"Mr Sallow?" Amanda's voice called from her office door as she appeared.

"Ah, Mandy, I've finished. Thank you very much."

"That's quite alright," Amanda brushed away his thanks gently. "Will Mr Acton be gracing us with a visit?" she asked hopefully for Robert's sake.

"No, not this time." Robert gave a small smile. "He's just got back from Japan."

"It was nice of him to check in on you." Amanda smiled back though she watched Robert with a concerned eye. "I do hope that his work will let him have some time off."

"Ah, that won't happen anytime soon." Robert smiled reminiscently. "It's tough at the top … besides, he's just like me."

"It can't be doing him any good-"

"He's happy," Robert interjected, looking to bring the topic to a close. "If you want him to consider visiting more, then let's work out where we are going to build this summerhouse."

"Robert!" Amanda exclaimed with a mock scowl on her face; she wagged a short, plump finger at him. "You know the answer! Now, away with you before you think up any more impossible requests."

Robert chuckled heartily as he held up a hand in defeat and strode away as best he could without tripping up on his walking stick.

This morning had played out differently from its usual routine due to Barry spending the day out with his family. Although Robert had maintained stretching his brain cells with the daily crossword, Martin's phone call had called him away at the same opportune moment that the Hughes family arrived to see John.

Back in his room, Robert placed his walking stick against the wall by the door, ready for when he left again later. Then he turned his attention fully to his record player. Caressing gentle fingers through his collection, he pulled out a record dedicated to Debussy. Carefully setting up the player, he eased himself into his armchair, ready to succumb to the musical delights. His fingers were twitching along with imaginary flute keys as he fondly remembered performing the same solos.

"Rob?" Mike's voice aroused Robert from his reverie. He opened his eyes as they focused through the light-filled room to see John in the doorway, Mike escorting his wheelchair.

"You mind some company, Pal? The Hughes rabble have left, and I could do with some relaxation myself."

"Come on in," Robert grinned, beckoning him over as he got up to reposition his armchair to make more room. "Make yourself at home."

"Do either of you want anything? Cup of tea?" Mike asked as he engaged the brakes on the wheelchair.

"A coffee would be lovely, thank you," Robert remarked, settling back into his chair.

John nodded in agreement before Mike disappeared. "So then, which great master is it today?"

"Debussy," Robert beamed. "And yes, I'm actually playing in this recording."

"I thought so; there's something about your playing. I'd like to think I could pick you out from any old orchestra but don't hold me to it." John chuckled as best as the right side of his face could demonstrate.

"How's Julia? And young Samuel?"

"Samuel is driving his mother up the wall with all his questions. Inquisitive lad; reminds me of myself. Julia, Och! She's not so little now. She's expecting in a couple of weeks, though what with dealing with the energy Sammie has, I'm surprised she hasn't popped prematurely!"

"Another little ginger nut to add to the Hughes biscuit tin?"

They both laughed before John remarked, "Baby might surprise us yet and be a custard cream like me son-in-law … then we'll be having an anaemic ginger-nut joining our clan!"

All jokes aside, John relayed the family gossip and updates as Robert listened eagerly, getting up only once to flip over the record before settling back down. The summer sun warmed the room lazily as they both melted comfortably into their chairs. Mike appeared with coffee and left again with a promise to check up on them again soon.

John's eyes eventually settled on the object beside the sideboard underneath the window. "You play chess?"

"What? Oh, yes. Well, not as much as I would like." Robert turned his head to look at the chess table in question. "Did you want a game? I thought it was a different intellect to your usual style."

"Nonsense! Drag it over here!" John's eyes sparkled.

Obligingly, Robert pulled the wooden table over and began pulling the pieces out of the drawer, offering the choice of colour to John before setting them up neatly on their respective squares.

"Rob?" Mike knocked as he walked into the room.

"Back so soon?" Robert commented with a welcoming smile, leaning back into his chair to see his visitor better.

"I'm sorry to bother you. Jean from room eight, down the corridor, asks if you'd mind playing Bach?"

"Of course." Robert's smile grew just a little as his heart warmed at the request.

Mike thanked him and left as Robert pulled himself out of his chair and began perusing his collection of records.

"Do you get many requests?" John asked humbly.

"Not necessarily, but I'm happy to oblige. Usually, it's Norma from room twelve who requests Jouvet. I don't really mind either way, as long as I'm making someone happy."

"You should host a record night and take requests."

"Amanda mentioned something similar once. Unfortunately, my collection is rather limited, so I declined. It would be a novelty lost sooner than my current request system allows."

John nodded in contemplated agreement and waited patiently for Robert to take his seat again before resuming the chess game. John easily took a strong lead against Robert's out-of-practice hand.

"I remember playing chess at university; I was studying for my doctorate at the time," John spoke aloud vaguely. "It was against a new upstart student, with every piece lost resulting in a dram of whisky," he smiled to himself.

"Do you want a tot?" Robert asked mischievously.

"What?" John snapped his full attention to his playmate.

"A tot! A dram! A tipple! Name it what you like, man, but do you want to raise the stakes?"

"We can't?" John sounded unsure, though he found himself leaning forward towards Robert's beaming grin and winking eye.

"We can …" Robert slowly stretched out a hand to the sideboard and opened the door, revealing a couple of bottles clearly marked The Macallan.

"You naughty boy! Rob, my pal, you're on!" John grinned lopsidedly as he looked up at his friend's dangerous smirk.

Ensuring their coffee mugs were drained clean, Robert cracked open one of the bottles, sniffing temptingly at the warm aroma wafting from the bottle top. He poured a small drop into each of their mugs, and the game resumed.

"It's a good job you're here today with me, chap. I was wondering how I was going to drink it all before Babs found out where I hid my reserve."

"Well, shh," John pursed his lips with a shaky finger. "She might find out yet if you're not quiet!"

"Hello, boys. Can I get you anything?" a voice called cheerily from the doorway.

"Jesus Christ Almighty!" Robert choked on the sip from his mug. "Ashley, where in God's name did you come from?" He craftily lowered his mug down the side of his chair closest to the window.

"Umm … I work here …?" Ashley eyed them both suspiciously.

"It's just chess, Lass!" John pronounced carefully. "It's all about strategy; a lot of thinking, and you startled us!"

"I'm sorry," Ashley replied quickly. "But can I get you anything?" she asked more slowly.

"Not a bean," John giggled to himself.

"We're alright, thank you," Robert answered, never taking his eyes off her lithe figure surrounded by the waterfall of silver braids.

"If you say so …" She turned slowly, and with a final glance at the two, she disappeared further down the corridor.

"Och, that wasn't funny!" John laughed loudly, whacking his right hand upon his knee in breathlessness.

"No, it wasn't! You're absolutely right there, chap," Robert laughed along with him, their voices filling the room completely.

With mutual agreement, the remainder of the whisky bottle was hidden back away, and the chess game continued until John, clearly pleased with himself, called out 'Checkmate.'

❁ ❁ ❁

That evening as the sunlight's fading embers covered the garden outside in a warm honey glow, John and Robert held back their laughter knowingly as Barbara brought up the topic of whisky from her usual knitting needle throne by the window in the Sun Lounge.

"You've been up to mischief," Dorothy whispered from beside Robert on the sofa.

"I'll invite you next time," Robert gently patted her hand with a wink.

"I should hope so!" she squeaked as she gently rested her head on his shoulder and closed her eyes.

Barry appeared in the doorway; his cheeks flushed with a rosy tint, and a large smile graced his face.

"Welcome back, Lad." John waved his right hand enthusiastically. "Did you miss us?"

"Of course." Barry sat down eagerly. "It was such a lovely day!"

"I don't think he missed us that much," Robert commented to John quietly as Barry enthusiastically regaled his day out with his family.

John listened intently and asked frequent questions, prompting Barry's grin to stretch further, all too happy to share his family's wedding exploits in the summer sun. Robert nodded now and then with a small smile in response. However, he could feel fatigue catching up with him. His head felt heavy and his bones weary, though he felt warmth from deep inside as he closed his eyes. Leaning his head against Dorothy's as he listened to Barry's deep baritone voice, his breathing slowing to match hers as he, too, fell asleep.

CHAPTER 9

AGED 90

Robert was hesitant to leave his room this morning. He sat in his armchair, staring out of the window, absently watching the autumnal breeze play with the trees outside. He picked up the card that sat on the sideboard next to him and reread the contents inside. It had arrived the day before from Martin, the words forming a brief essay of mixed congratulations and apologies for not being able to celebrate his birthday in person with him.

With a small smile, Robert placed the card back. He sighed as he once again noted that Martin, a man twenty years his junior, had never forgotten his birthday. In fact, no one here at Mimosa Grange had ever forgotten. The residents may have their special quirks and oddities, but they maintained an extended family feel; no one was ever left behind, not even himself.

With a resolute sigh, Robert placed his hands firmly down to push himself up and out of his armchair. There was no point dragging your feet when a man needed to eat. Clasping his walking stick deftly from its place near the door, he made his way downstairs to meet up with the others for breakfast.

Regardless of the importance of the date, the morning played out its usual daily routine. After breakfast, Robert led the way to the Sun Lounge, walking with Barry, who pushed John in his wheelchair. The three of them sat together as they tried to push the limits of their brains in the conundrums presented before them. Barbara's knitting needles provided a quiet backdrop from her usual corner by the window. Every now and then, her voice could be heard muttering about 'whisky weather' before her needles took up their rhythmic clacking once more.

During dinner, Robert found himself at the head of the table. His heart sank briefly as he recalled the unfortunate events at Dorothy's birthday. He took a deep breath, releasing his grip on his walking stick and resting it against the top of the table. He mustered a smile and pushed his memories back as Barry and John joined him.

"Ta-da!" John shakingly pulled out a garish party hat that was tucked down beside him and held it out to Robert. "The birthday lad needs a hat."

Barry made sure the wheelchair's brakes were firmly applied before he sat on the other side of John, just as Barbara took her place at the other end of the table.

"Now, don't tell me," she leaned forward as far as she could with a mischievous grin, "you have some of that special reserve ready to celebrate tonight."

"You'll have to wait and find out!" Robert whispered back with a wink.

Barbara pulled back with a pout, but she declined to make her usual fuss in case the expected tot of whisky never made its way to her at all.

Dinner was a delicious blend of hearty stew and rustic farmhouse bread. The room was filled with the usual moans and groans intermingled with the laughter and good cheer from Robert's table. Barry was regaling a tale from the first time he had met Robert whilst John slapped the arm of his wheelchair, gasping for air through his raucous laughter.

"Where is he?" An unexpected yell subdued the room. "Where's the birthday boy?"

"Ma'am, please keep the noise down; we need to respect the other residents." Amanda's authoritative voice soon followed as she appeared beside a couple in the doorway.

"Ah, I see him!" the woman shrieked again as she teetered her way over to Robert on obnoxiously high heels. "Happy birthday, Dad!"

"… Lisa?" Robert sat up straight and dropped his hand to find the comforting grip of his walking stick.

"Lisa!" Barry, John and Barbara all mouthed silently to each other, wide-eyed, as they, too, pulled back to watch the scene unfolding before them.

"Let's get a picture then!" Lisa held her mobile in front of their faces as she placed herself almost on top of Robert. Her perfume was chokingly heavy. As soon as she had put her face next to his, she had pulled back to inspect the resulting photo and discuss it with her husband, who had sulked in behind her.

The room regained some of its usual chatter as the excitement of having visitors abated.

"Oh, Kevin, look at this dreadful cardigan he's wearing!" She was pointing emphatically at the phone screen in her hand.

Her husband agreed though his face remained fixed in its uninterested state as he began to watch the latest match on his own mobile.

"Well, as luck would have it …!" Her toothy grin unnerved all sat at the table as she shimmied a package in a ridiculous fashion in front of Robert before placing it in his hands rather decidedly.

Robert stared at the glittery mass before him. The paper felt just as unnatural as it looked and was already irritating the skin on his hands.

"Go ahead, open it!" Lisa urged as she thrust her mobile in front of him again. Her nails, as loud as her shoes, curled around the device haphazardly. Her impatience getting the better of her, she thrust her free hand towards him to start unwrapping the bundle. "Here, let me help."

Robert twisted his face away as she began to claw at the package, muttering curses. He winced as the package dropped down on his hands again, a slither of torn material clutched in between her fingers.

"There, that's started it for you. It's my fault for wrapping it so well." She laughed aloud at herself.

Gingerly, Robert continued to peel back the paper, swallowing his trepidation as the item was being revealed. The woollen fabric of a dirty cream jumper began to emerge.

Lisa snatched it up and held it up for everyone to see. "Doesn't it just scream you?" She held it up against him as he tilted his head back out of the way, swallowing once more where the fabric pressed against his throat. She whipped it away and thrust it into her husband's hands, forcing him to reangle his own mobile to continue watching the match.

"Let's take this awful one off, and you can wear your nice new one," Lisa began roughly holding up the end of his cardigan sleeve and, shaking his arm up and down in the process, made him remove his own arm. It took no time at all for her to whisk the sleeve off his other side and remove the garment altogether. Thrusting the jumper over his head, Robert soon found himself dressed again, this time in the ill-fitting scratchy wool. His head struggled to catch up with the whirlwind around him as Lisa brandished her mobile once again, tapping viciously at the screen as various clicking noises issued from the device.

He was rather glad when Jessica approached with her tray of birthday cupcakes. He caught a glimpse of the spongey delights before the tray was placed down on the table next to his. He already knew what flavours they were from his lengthy discussions with the Lewis couple. He had asked for coffee and walnut, carrot cake, Victoria sponge, red velvet, and chocolate. His cake demands were purely so he could enjoy the faces of the other residents as they sampled their favourite flavours without the hassle of inches of sugary icing. A small smile began to grace his lips as his heart warmed with the effort Jessica had put into making his request a reality.

This was short-lived. Robert's smile faded as he watched his daughter's reaction before him.

"Oh, goodness! What is this?"

"Cupcakes for all the residents in celebration of Rob's birthday." Jessica raised an eyebrow at the question. "Is there a problem?"

"Oh, you needn't have bothered. Well, it looks like you haven't. They're hardly decorated! It doesn't matter; I brought my own." Lisa turned sharply to her husband and began fussing over the bag he had plonked on the floor at his feet, still transfixed on the screen in his hands.

Ignoring the comments just passed, Jessica turned to Robert. "What flavour would you like?"

"Chocolate, please." he smiled at her gratefully.

"You don't want that, Dad!" Lisa moved the cupcake placed in front of him and dumped a box down in its place. "You want one of *these*!" she emphasised as she removed the lid, revealing hard icing and vibrant sugary colours that made Robert's stomach turn.

Without waiting for his reply, Lisa continued taking numerous selfies with him, posing with various grins about his head.

Jessica bit down on her tongue hard as she continued to share her cupcakes with the rest of the room. Gracious replies of thanks from the residents helped her to hold her words and tears back.

Enough was enough. Robert stood abruptly, clutching onto his walking stick. "I'm going to use the facilities," he uttered in Lisa's direction before he made his exit.

He chewed his bottom lip as he tapped his way along the corridor. Despite his slower pace, he made a beeline for anywhere that was far enough away. A thought suddenly jolted him to a stop in his tracks. *Dorothy. Where was she?* He swallowed hard as he cast his mind back. She was normally late to the dining hall for dinner, but had she snuck in whilst Lisa had occupied his time? He looked back behind him, contemplating returning to check. *No, I'm sure she wasn't there!* Panic squeezed his heart as he set his focus on his destination.

"Rob!" Mike greeted him in the corridor outside of Dorothy's room.

"Is she here? Where is she? How is she?" Robert gasped heavily; his legs ached from over-exertion.

"She's here and resting," Mike smiled and blinked his watery eyes.

"Can I go in?" Robert tried not to choke on his words.

"Of course!"

Mike followed Robert into the room and pulled the armchair into place next to Dorothy's bedside. He helped

Robert sit down and ensured he was comfortable, gently relieving him of his stick and leaning it against the wall. "I'll be back in a minute."

Robert nodded his thanks before turning his attention to Dorothy. Her frail shrunken frame was obscured in layers of blankets as she slept. Her face looked pale. Not wishing to wake her, Robert hesitated on what to do. His mind flashed back to her one-hundredth birthday when she held his hand.

Pushing the bed sheet back slightly to reveal her hand, he encased it in both of his.

Her cold, delicate, bony fingers twitched slightly as his warmth slowly seeped into her skin. Her eyes flickered as she took a deep intake of breath. "Rob...ert."

"My dear Dorothy." He smiled at her, gently stroking her hand in his. "What's this all about then? Are you trying to get back at me for how I behaved at your centenary?"

She chuckled faintly before coughing, raising her other hand slowly to cover her mouth. She closed her eyes for a moment and then dragging her hand back down beneath the sheets; Robert lifted them slightly to aid her, tucking them under her chin.

Her icy grey eyes found him again as she smiled. Her face twisted as her eyes narrowed, transfixed on his jumper. Puzzled, he glanced down and frowned at the fabric hanging loosely from him. He withdrew his hands reluctantly though he felt the overbearing need to rid himself of this godforsaken jumper.

"You wouldn't believe me if I told you what happened today." He looked up at her before continuing to pull and tug at the sleeves. Eventually, the fabric relinquished its grip on him. In a fit of frustration, he held his arm high, about to throw the garment as far as he could … However, he slowly brought his arm back down and began to gently fold the jumper. Despite its newness, the fabric was itchy. The branded labels had scratched the back of his neck, and the glitter residue from the wrapping paper was getting everywhere, glinting annoyingly at him as it caught the light.

He snorted in dismay before placing it gently on the sideboard in front of him.

His eyes sought Dorothy's again as he carefully placed her hand between his. She smiled at him once again with a small squeak of contentment.

"Rotten jumper," he mumbled, "but still, she gave it to me." He took a deep breath. "Lisa came today. My daughter. For the first time since I arrived here … She came to see me …" He shook his head with anxious laughter. "No, I know, she didn't come here to see me. I've been assaulted by a whirlwind, and I still can't believe what I just went through!

"She took all manner of photos from that stupid device they call a mobile nowadays. She undressed me and shoved that godforsaken jumper on me. I've never been so embarrassed!" He leaned forward closer to Dorothy's ear. "Even at the young age of ninety, I've never had the staff dress me here … Well, apart from Mike once, but he got the raw end of the deal having to put my socks on!"

Dorothy giggled softly as he continued.

"Then Jess came in with those marvellous cupcakes she makes. Oh, you should have seen them: all sorts of flavours, a right menagerie it was … And that stupid girl … the audacity she has to be so rude! Poor Jess. I couldn't stand it anymore, so I left … I just walked away, Dorothy … I walked away."

Robert's head hung low, bent double with his forehead pressing against their hands; his voice became distant. "The hateful creature I am wishes she had just forgotten all about me … like I already believed … She signed all the papers to put me here, took me away from my home and left me to rot where she couldn't see me … And yet I can't bring myself to throw away … that godforsaken … jumper!"

Dorothy squeezed his hand weakly. Pulling her other hand out from the covers once more, she reached over to place it unceremoniously on his head. Robert jumped slightly but stayed where he was as her feathery touch stroked his thin hair comfortingly.

"It takes strength … to walk away …" she breathed softly.

Robert could hear her smile as he closed his eyes momentarily to absorb her pure essence. "And it is an awful jumper!" She burst out into silent giggles.

Robert lifted his head, chuckling with her. She began coughing again and withdrew her hand from his head to cover her mouth as her body convulsed involuntarily. Pulling his handkerchief from his pocket, he stretched forward and dabbed at the corners of her mouth. Her coughing fit subsided, and she smiled at him with exhausted eyes.

In return, Robert tucked her free hand back under the blankets and gently smoothed back a lock of her hair that had dislodged from the top of her head and stuck to the clammy sweat of her forehead.

"How about you just rest your eyes for a bit," Robert soothed. "I won't leave your side."

Dorothy nodded faintly before broken, heavy breaths issued from her lips. He watched her solemnly as her chest heaved up and down, her frail hand still resting in his. It wasn't long before his own eyes were threatening to close.

The room was dark when Robert eventually awoke. He fidgeted in his seat, causing the blanket that had been placed over him to fall into his lap. In an attempt to rearrange it, he pulled his arm back, realising slowly that Dorothy's hand was still nestled in his.

"Dorothy!" he exclaimed with a whisper. Panic rose within him as he forgot about the blanket and leaned forward on the edge of the armchair. "Dorothy?" he pleaded gently, half expecting the worst.

She smiled weakly at the familiar voice calling her name, her fingers twitching in his palm, though she remained silent and still.

Leaning forward, he gently dabbed at the pearls of cold sweat shining in the moonlight that peered in through the window. He lifted her hand in both of his and kissed her delicate knuckles before resting his forehead against their joined hands. His heart weighed heavily, tightening in his chest.

A knock at the door made Robert pull back with a stretch and straighten himself to sit comfortably in the chair once more. Mike entered the room, carrying a small plate with a handful of cupcakes towered upon it and Robert's fleece cardigan folded over his arm.

"You're awake," Mike gave a small smile. "How you feeling?"

"Old … What time is it?" Robert watched as Mike placed the plate down and turned on the lamp, dimly lighting the room in a warm glow.

"Just gone two in the morning. Jess told me what happened. Thought you might be wanting this as well as the blanket." Mike held up the cardigan, ready for Robert to slip his arms through. Robert willingly obliged; he had felt a chill creep upon him with only his shirt on his back.

"I didn't know what flavour you wanted, so I brought one of each." Mike ran a hand awkwardly across the back of his head with a sheepish grin. "Amanda asked your daughter to leave. She gave your excuses very diplomatically."

"I must find a way to make up for my daughter's behaviour today. She was incredibly rude, and I didn't stand up to her. I let her get away with it. I'm sorry."

"There's no need to apologise on her behalf. We care about you and want to make sure you feel safe. The same goes for all the residents here." Mike gave Robert's shoulder a small reassuring squeeze. "I would ask if you want to head back to your own room, but I think we both know the answer."

"I couldn't leave her." Robert glanced back at Dorothy. Her breathing was becoming more rapid, and her fragile frame was shivering. "Dorothy?"

Her face contorted with pain again. Robert picked up her hand and gently stroked the clammy skin of her arm as he tried to comfort her.

"I'll call for the doctor," Mike called over his shoulder as he disappeared into the corridor.

"Now then." Robert's voice was shaky. "The doctor will be here soon, and he'll help manage that pain for you. You'll be able to have a good night's sleep, and you'll feel better in the morning, you'll see."

He dabbed at her forehead, gently stroking her cheek before running his hand down the length of her arm again. He patted her hand gently as he began to ramble. "Mike brought some of Jess's cakes up for you to see. We can have them for breakfast in the morning; you'll feel better then."

He paused to fold his handkerchief and reapply it to the pearls of sweat forming again. "Dorothy?"

No reply, no gentle squeeze from her delicate hand.

"Dorothy!" Robert cried. "No, no, no … I can't live without you!" He clutched desperately at her hand as it fell, limp and heavy. "My dear Dorothy … You can't leave me … I'm not strong enough … to walk away … not from you."

A single tear escaped from her eye as her breathing slowed to a stop.

CHAPTER 10

AGED 91

Outside, the mimosas were in full bloom, scattering the garden in a brilliant sea of vibrant sunshine yellow. Sat in his armchair, Robert's eyes gazed lazily through his bedroom window, watching the gentle spring breeze dance amongst the flowers. His heart, on the other hand, was heavy as he absent-mindedly played with the chocolate lime in his cardigan pocket.

"Why me, Dorothy?" he began to whisper to himself. "Why did you hold on to me and give me that chocolate lime on my first day here? How did you know how much I needed you? I've been told I'm nothing like your brother; we don't share a name or even look similar … Are you with him now?"

He sighed as he fiddled with the ends of the plastic packaging. "Do you know how hard it has been? You left me without a word. Not even goodbye. You didn't leave any kind words, not even in a will … There is nothing left of you apart from the shadow of your footsteps across my heart."

He closed his eyes as the memories flooded his thoughts.

On that day, he couldn't bring himself to get out of bed. Ashley knocked at the door as she came in, perching on the end of his bed.

"I thought you would like these," her voice soothed as she pulled a small white paper bag out of her pocket and placed it in his hand. She watched him for a moment before giving his leg a reassuring pat and leaving. He slowly looked down at the bag, his body aching as realisation dawned on him. Hesitantly he opened it. The sight of the glistening hard, green, boiled sweets caused his heart to drop. He slowly unwrapped one and popped it into his mouth. He savoured every second as it gradually melted to reveal its chocolate centre, coating his cold cheeks with warm salty tears.

❋❋❋

"There are so many things I wanted to ask; I should have asked you … why didn't I ask you?" He continued to whisper to himself as he tapped a fist repeatedly against the arm of his chair. "I wanted to know more about you, your brother, your family. What other memories did you share with your brother other than chocolate limes? What was he like? I know nothing … yet, you know nothing of me … I guess we're in the same boat, aren't we?

"I wanted to tell you, but I didn't know how. I would have told you about growing up in Bourneville. How I got my scholarship. All the places around this world that I've seen, the concert halls and the music. I would have told you everything … if you wanted to listen … I'd listen to you …"

He stared out at the mimosa blooms again as they waved back. Swallowing hard, he continued. "I wanted to tell you about Linda. I think, of all people, you would have understood. I haven't even told Martin … but you, you made me want to share all my secrets … You made me believe that my past transgressions were forgiven …

"I met Linda at a theatre hall where I would be performing. She worked there, and I guess one thing led to another, and we were soon married. It was just as I was starting to build fame for my own compositions. The world called to me, and we needed the money with Lisa on the way. I know I wasn't the most attentive husband and father, and the marriage fell apart … well, I was never home … but Linda was always friendly to me … we were always amicable. I gave money to her for Lisa for as long as I can remember, and she kept me updated. Though our relationship lasted, my relationship with Lisa became almost non-existent. She didn't even tell me about her wedding with Kevin … Linda did. She thought I ought to know …

"I'm rambling, I know, but you see … despite everything, I wasn't there when Linda passed. I didn't know until five years later. For my sins of living my career with every breath and soul, I couldn't even say goodbye to my friend. And for what damage I've caused to my relationship with my daughter … I swear I never instilled her attitude towards money; I wasn't there enough to do so … I don't believe her mother did either. But, nonetheless, she kept her own mother's death away from me … It was because she feared the money would stop…

"I suppose it's karma or divine retribution … As much as I always regretted what led up to this, I find it laughable that I actually stopped the payments … I don't think I would have stopped if she had told me the truth. I can't say I feel betrayed, but … I guess … that was the first time I fully opened my eyes to the person my daughter had become …"

He suddenly closed his eyes tight and placed a cold hand against his heart, the other gripping the chocolate lime firmly in his pocket. "Oh, my sweet, dear Dorothy. Don't think for a second that you were ever a replacement for the loneliness I brought upon myself. Though at one point I did indeed love Linda, my feelings for you have always encompassed me, body and soul. You constantly surprised me with how you could make me exceed my limitations. You pushed me further than even I could push myself … Do you even know how lost I am … without you …?"

Robert sighed as he wiped at the escaping tears. "Since you first caught my arm in your delicate hand, you turned this prison cell of an institute, this harbinger of death, into a home. A home with love and joy. My darkest days were turned into hopeful light. But then you … you left me … I wasn't strong enough to walk away from you, yet you left me behind instead. I finally understand how music could die. You still managed to teach me something new … but it hurts,

Dorothy. Your absence hurts. Did you know it would be like this? Why didn't you tell me? Why did you cause me so much pain, and yet I love you even more for it? I miss you …"

He took a deep breath, his long-held burdens slowly releasing in the vision of her imprinted on the back of his eyelids. Slowly he opened his eyes again, blinking back the rest of the tears with his red, puffy eyes and wiping his nose with his handkerchief. Twisting in his chair, he reached over and carefully opened the flute case where it lived upon the sideboard, shakily lifting out each part and assembling his cherished instrument. He ran his fingers over the keys with a sad reminiscence. His travel companion for so many years as they performed across the world, playing from the great classical masters to his own compositions; they had been inseparable.

With a deep intake of breath, he raised his flute to his lips. A crystal note filled the room as he began to play the Parting Glass, the music filling his room and sailing down the corridors.

John, who had suffered another major stroke within the last year, lay propped up in his bed. The notes filled his lungs with renewed breath as he conducted vaguely with his left hand. His mouth struggled to voice the words silently as he sang to his heart's content in his mind. Julia sat beside him, gently rocking her two-year-old daughter in her arms. Samuel was reading in the corner quietly. Every now and then, he looked up to observe his family before continuing.

Further down the corridor, Barry's children had come to visit. Despite their busy schedules, both David and Mary pulled out all the stops to see their father together once a month; they also came separately more frequently. As the music flowed faintly around his room, Barry paused mid-sentence, walked over to his nightstand where Mathilda's photo took pride of place and gently caressed her face.

Barbara's knitting needles could be heard from her room on the other side of the corridor as they slowed to a pace that matched the music. She hummed broken phrases in between counting her stitches as a small smile graced her rosy face.

Ashley and Mike happened to be on shift together today, the sound of Robert's flute reaching them in broken refrains as they bustled around their daily duties. Every now and then, they stopped with a worried glance at each other as the music became overly breathy or paused longer than expected between verse and chorus.

As Robert played, his mind filled with images of Dorothy. Her angelic disposition as she wheeled her Zimmer frame around her usual route of Mimosa Grange on her daily walks. The squeaks of excitement at his antics and the smile she reserved just for him.

Deftly he transitioned straight into Dorothy's Birthday Symphony, hoping with every note that she could hear him. His lungs burned, and his arms were becoming heavier with exhaustion. He closed his eyes, concentrating on each note and then the next. His heart tightened as he pushed himself further, frustration beginning to grip him as the end of the piece seemed further away with each breath.

With an anguished sigh, he dropped his arms and flute into his lap. His head dropped back to rest against the armchair as he sighed once more; *he couldn't finish playing yet again.*

He lolled his head to one side to gaze aimlessly out of the doorway where the radio at the nurse's station could be heard. His latest composition, An Angel's Ghost, could be heard weaving its way through the corridor and into the resident's rooms. He followed every note with welling tears. Martin had found excellent musicians to bring out the emotions the piece deserved. He absently slipped his hand into his pocket and found the chocolate lime secured there.

A faint figure ambled past his doorway, stopped, and retraced its steps to watch fondly towards where he sat. His heart skipped. He could feel every beat louder than the last as it began to race against his chest.

"My dear Dorothy!" he smiled lovingly as her warmth filled him. Raising himself out of his chair to greet her, he felt lighter. After so long, he could finally breathe again in her presence.

CHAPTER 11

PRESENT DAY

66 To Lisa, I leave to you my memories …" Mr Wright coughed, shuffling the papers in his hands; his eyes watched Lisa cautiously as he continued to read out the will.

"To Amanda Doherty, a formidable woman who always ensures the best for her residents. I know, through our numerous conversations over the years, money doesn't stretch far in a high-quality place such as Mimosa Grange. I have pestered you and caused you more trouble than it's worth in regards to a summerhouse, but I still maintain that such a beautiful garden should be experienced and enjoyed. Hence, I leave to you five hundred thousand pounds to bring our years of discussion to a final fruition. I trust you will spend it wisely. I also leave my records and record player to all the residents, present and future, of Mimosa Grange. Just in case you dare to forget me, Mandy."

Lisa's eyes narrowed scathingly at Amanda as she bit down hard on her bottom lip.

Mr Wright observed silently, throwing a raised eyebrow at Martin sitting beside him as he continued. "To Mike Smith, a man I have learned to depend on for more than just delivering my letters, I leave to you and your darling daughter, Amiyah, my most treasured companion, my flute. I cannot take my dear friend with me, and after my fall, you both showed such dedication to looking after my flute until you reunited us. I have also had words with an old associate at the Royal College of Music. Amiyah, if you continue to forge down the path of classical music as determinedly as you do now, then your scholarship is reserved financially by myself in a trust fund. It is also stipulated that if, at the time of choosing your career, you travel down a different path, then the College reserves the right to use the money to sponsor another gifted student. I also hope that, if my wishes are followed accordingly, and you are all together right now, you will take the opportunity to get Martin's number after the reading."

Lisa's eyes were now directed at Mike, who stood awkwardly at the back of the room. She grimaced as she watched him run a hand across the back of his head embarrassedly. He was looking at Martin, who waved knowingly back at him.

"To Ashley and Jessica Lewis." Mr Wright directed the attention back on to himself, "I leave to you two hundred thousand pounds as a housewarming gift. The property ladder is not a kind one, but I hope this helps you take the first step out of the damp basement you have continued to suffer for so long."

Ashley's hands flew to her open mouth in surprise. Jessica hugged her tightly as they listened further.

"I also leave to you one hundred thousand pounds and my warmest wishes as you begin to expand your family."

One of Ashley's hands dropped to her lower abdomen, the tears welling uncontrollably. Jessica hugged her tighter and kissed her neon-green highlighted chestnut hair.

With her arms firmly crossed and her teeth gritted tightly through a mixture of despair and frustration, Mr Wright watched as Lisa mouthed silent curses.

"To Barry Walker, I hope you forgive me, for I have already acted upon your gift. In fact, I acted upon this over six years ago. I donated fifty thousand pounds to a charity that helps research dementia in their search for better understanding and, hopefully, an eventual cure. I did this under the name of Mathilda Walker."

Barry clapped his hands together in a shaky prayer, rocking gently back and forward as he professed his thanks.

Lisa's long, manicured nails were chaotically drumming against her arm as she chewed at her bottom lip. Her husband, Kevin, glanced up from his phone nonchalantly before ignoring her and his surroundings again.

"To John Hughes, I leave to you my chessboard. Though it is not the same as the daily crossword we shared each morning, the rare occasions on which we did play were most enjoyable. I hope you can enjoy this strategic game with your grandson for many years to come.

"To Barbara Tuffin, I leave to you my bottle of thirty-year-old The Macallan whisky. I sincerely hope you don't give your son too much trouble over it, for which I apologise in advance."

From his wheelchair beside Barry, John smiled crookedly, nodding his head knowingly; grateful, though all capacity to speak was currently absent. Barbara, on the other hand, was expressing her gratitude very raucously. Her grin stretched from ear to ear as she savoured the thought of the taste. She had waited a long time to feel the smooth liquid of a vintage whisky again.

Mr Wright called for quiet before clearing his throat and continuing. "To Martin Acton, the son I never had ..."

A scornful scoff could be heard from Lisa's direction.

Mr Wright raised an eyebrow but nevertheless carried on. "I leave to you all the royalties for any and all of my compositions. You have shared my career and surpassed me. I am fortunate that, during my years here at Mimosa Grange, you are just as much, if not more so, of a workaholic as me. Through the help of our mutual acquaintance, Mike, I have been able to send you score after score of music that documented my emotional rollercoaster of a life. But it all comes down to your hard work, knowledge and effort that made them all such successes. You deserve to reap the reward you helped me sow. Thank you, my boy.

"Finally, to my daughter Lisa ..."

At the mention of her name, her legs uncrossed as she leaned forward from her perch at the edge of her seat, her heels clicking on the floor as she did so.

"Along with my memories, I also bequeath unto you the jumper I couldn't bring myself to throw away. I know I have not been the father you wanted, but just maybe, I was the father you deserved. I may not always like you or the choices you make … however, I have never stopped loving you, my little girl."

Mr Wright placed his papers back into his briefcase and produced a box from beside his chair, holding it out towards Lisa.

She leapt up from her chair and snatched at the box. "This has to be a joke!" she muttered under her breath as she tore away the lid and tissue paper. She pulled out the dirty cream knitted jumper with its labels still in place. In frantic desperation, she tugged and pulled, thoroughly inspecting every inch and fold of the fabric until finally, she revealed the last remaining piece of Robert … one chocolate lime.